From Hero To Racer

PRAISE FOR *STORYSHARES*

"One of the brightest innovators and game-changers in the education industry."
– Forbes

"Your success in applying research-validated practices to promote literacy serves as a valuable model for other organizations seeking to create evidence-based literacy programs."

- Library of Congress

"We need powerful social and educational innovation, and Storyshares is breaking new ground. The organization addresses critical problems facing our students and teachers. I am excited about the strategies it brings to the collective work of making sure every student has an equal chance in life."
– Teach For America

"Around the world, this is one of the up-and-coming trailblazers changing the landscape of literacy and education."
- International Literacy Association

"It's the perfect idea. There's really nothing like this. I mean wow, this will be a wonderful experience for young people."   - Andrea Davis Pinkney, Executive Director, Scholastic

"Reading for meaning opens opportunities for a lifetime of learning. Providing emerging readers with engaging texts that are designed to offer both challenges and support for each individual will improve their lives for years to come. Storyshares is a wonderful start."
- David Rose, Co-founder of CAST & UDL

From Hero To Racer

Matthias and Nancy Southwick

STORYSHARES

Story Share, Inc.
New York. Boston. Philadelphia

Storyshares
Story Share, Inc.
24 N. Bryn Mawr Avenue #340
Bryn Mawr, PA 19010-3304
www.storyshares.org

Inspiring reading with a new kind of book.

Interest Level: High School
Grade Level Equivalent: 3.2

9781642611090

Book design by Storyshares

Printed in the United States of America

Storyshares Presents

1

I thought this was going to be a crappy move. Then we pulled up to the new house on moving day. My new neighbor across the street was working on a 05 Pontiac GTO.

"Dad, look at that awesome street racer!"

"Yeah, that's cool, Zack," Dad remarked.

My dad's not into cars as much as I am. I had less than a year until I could get my driver's license. It's all I could think about. I dreamt of being able to build my own car too. I just didn't have enough money to get started.

The neighbor's car wasn't anywhere near ready to race yet. It was still in pieces all over his garage. *I wondered if he would talk shop with me?*

I stared at the GTO every time I came to get another box. It was right there in front of me. Right across the street. I was getting tired of carrying boxes and looking at the GTO helped pass the time.

My new room looked out over the street. I had a perfect view of my neighbor's garage and that GTO. I was supposed to be setting up my room. Instead I was staring out the window.

Mom interrupted my daydreaming with a reminder to finish my room. "Didn't I hear about plans for a car show? I would like you to get your room done before then," Mom chuckled.

"Mom, that's not for another week yet!"

"I know, I know, but with all this daydreaming..."

"Dont worry, Mom, I'll get it done."

"If you say so," she laughed on her way out.

2

I managed to get my room finished before the car show. And yes, that was with plenty of daydreaming.

On the morning of the car show, breakfast seemed to take forever. All I wanted to do was leave. Dad was taking forever. Mom kept packing more stuff in the cooler for us.

"Please, can we leave now? Please!" I pleaded.

"Ok, Bud," Dad chuckled. "We're going."

We pulled up to the car show parking lot. Even some of the cars in the parking lot were cool. I couldn't wait to see the show cars.

That show was great! They had everything there! Old hot rods, dragsters, hooked up street cars, and show cars. I could have walked that place ten times and still not have been tired of it.

It was lunch time, so Dad and I headed for our car.

"Hey neighbor!" someone said. It was the GTO guy who lived across the street from us. "Hi, I'm Don. I live right across the street from you," he said. "This is my daughter, Ella. My wife Becky isn't here. She doesn't really care for cars."

"Hi, I'm Peter. This is my son Zack.," Dad said. "My wife Jenn usually comes along. But she is bent on getting everything unpacked."

"Are you guys car buffs like us?" Don asked. "Ella's only five and is already hooked on cars." Ella grinned widely, but sheepishly hugged her dad's leg.

"I do like the shows," Dad said. "But Zack here can't get enough of cars. We go to every car show in driving distance."

"I saw the GTO you're working on. Great car, and fast," I said.

"Thanks. It's a good car to get started with, because the parts are so cheap. I'm trying to get done in time for a race coming up. But I'm working by myself. I don't think I'll make it in time. I could really use your help. If you're allowed?"

"Yeah! I would love to!" I said as fast as I could.

"Yeah. Thats fine with me," Dad said.

"Great, I'll be home from work at 4:00," Don said.

We had plenty of food to share. So we invited Don and Ella to eat with us. They agreed to eat with us and we had a lot of fun. The four of us spent the rest of the day together.

3

I met Don after he got home from work the next day. The car needed a lot of work. Ella played in front of the garage while we worked. Don had a full roll cage installed inside. He also had the plastic interior parts and the back seats out.

Don said we could only change certain things. It was part of the rules for the racing series he liked. We started by unhooking everything we were allowed to change on the engine. Every once in a while, Ella would hand us tools we needed. We worked nonstop for several hours. When we realized it was really late, we called it quits for the night.

I went over to help again the following day. We started installing the new engine parts. It was harder putting parts back on than taking them off. At our speed, I could tell it would be weeks of work. A lot of it I'd already read about before. I get more than one car magazine in the mail.

Did I really need this hands on training?

4

I kept going to help Don. He was a cool guy and a good teacher. We were also getting to know one another while working. One day, he told me something I didn't expect.

"Here is the most important thing I can tell you. Keep the racing on the track. One of the worst mistakes I ever made was street racing."

"Why, did something happen?" I asked impatiently.

"Yeah. I was eighteen. I raced every chance I got. One time I was showing off and wrecked my car. It was a bad wreck. I almost ended up in a wheelchair. The good part, is that no one else got hurt. But, it's caused life-long problems for me."

"Like what?"

"Well, the main thing is pain. Pain every day. All day."

"You don't act like you're in pain."

"I take heavy pain meds every day. I would be stuck in bed without them. This is my first car built since then. It's painful. But it distracts me."

"Distracts you from what?"

"Becky and I had another child. She died. Her name was Emma. It's almost been two years, but it still hurts."

"Oh. I'm sorry. I didn't know." I looked over at Ella. She was playing jump rope at the edge of the garage.

"She was only three. She doesn't really remember. She knows her sister is in heaven. But that's about it."

"That's why you work on the car every day?"

"Yeah. It's rough going through all this pain. Knowing I won't even get to race it."

"What do you mean?" I asked, very puzzled.

"My wife said I'm not allowed to race again. She said she's too afraid she'll lose me. I've been trying to find a driver, but it's hard. Some drivers have a bad driving record. Some aren't aggressive enough to place. That means their time wasn't fast enough to be in the race..."

I couldn't help but drift off into thought. Could I be his driver?

5

I was glued to the computer. I read and read. There were dozens and dozens of different racing types. Each racing type had different rules listed. There's so much information on the internet, it's overwhelming. One article led to another and another. It was just too much. I needed a break. But I started reading again and that's when I found it.

NASCAR LOWERS DRIVING AGE FROM 16 to 15.

"YES! YES! WAHOO!" I couldnt help but shout aloud.

My mom came in to see what I was so excited about. I told her about Don looking for a driver. So she helped me do some more research. The allowable driving age depended on the group running the race. Don wanted to enter the IMSA Continental Tire Sports Car Challenge. IMSA stood for The International Motor Sports Association. The IMSA didn't have a minimum age requirement.

I would need to go to performance driving school. I would need to pass a physical. You had to be in good enough shape to handle long races. Then, I would need to file for membership in the IMSA. The first race in the series would be at NJ Motorsports Park.

First, I needed to figure out how to ask Don.

6

We were getting close to being done with the car. Don still hadn't found a driver. I wasn't sure how to start the conversation with him. 'I know I'm only fifteen, but, can I be your driver?' That's just not going to work. I think Don could tell I was distracted. But he didn't say anything right away.

We were installing aftermarket racing gages, because they are more accurate. Don was in the driver's seat. I was going back and forth for tools we needed. Ella usually helped us with the tools. But, she was distracted by a new ball. I stopped to watch her for a second. Trying to think of what to say to Don.

"Everything ok, Zack?" Don asked. Just then, Ella's ball bounced away from her into the street. She ran after it. A car was coming down the street. They were going way too fast and weren't looking.

"Ella! Stop!" I yelled. She didn't stop. I dropped the tool I was holding and made a dash for her. I snatched her out of the car's way just in time. The side view mirror just brushed my shirt. The car didn't even stop. Don was right behind me. He grabbed me and Ella, hugging us both tight. Becky had heard me yell Ella's name and came running out.

Out of nowhere I had a camera crew in my face. "That was incredible! What's your name young man?"

7

"Kim Sutherland here, with Channel 8 News. We are live on the scene with 15-year-old, Zack Wilton, whose daring rescue we accidentally caught on film just moments ago. We were here doing a piece on a historical landmark. What a double whammy. Talk about us both being in the right place at the right time. How do you feel about being a hero, Zack?"

"Great, I guess." I wasn't sure what to say. I didn't feel any different than I did earlier.

"You just risked your life to save five-year-old Ella. Did you think about it or was it just instinct?"

"I didn't really think about it. I just know how much she means to her parents."

"Well, a great job you did young man. For those of you just joining us..."

My parents were standing with us now. They couldn't stop grinning from ear to ear. Don and Becky couldn't stop hugging Ella. After the camera crew was done, they all gave me big hugs.

"We can't thank you enough for what you did. Anything you want, just name it and it's yours," Don said.

I knew exactly what I wanted to ask for. "I would like to be your driver for the Continental Challenge."

"Well, we had better get that car done then. We need to get you to driving school."

8

The next two weeks were hectic and exhausting. We had tons to do in a short amount of time. I couldn't register until I passed the performance driving school. We had a few tasks to complete before that could happen. One, I needed the GTO finished for driving school. Two, I had never driven before.

My dad borrowed a friend's car with a manual transmission. We went to an empty parking lot almost every day. It was much easier than I thought to drive stick shift. I had it down pat in only a few tries. I also had to do a few TV interviews about saving Ella. But I did those during the day while Don was at work. The good part was, the publicity helped us land some sponsors.

Don and I worked every day on the car. We had to make sure it was running at peak performance.

It got done much quicker once Don called his friend Ezariah Jackson. He liked to be called Ez. Ez owned a small race course in the area, Jackson Raceway. Ez volunteered to be the crew chief for crew Wilton. In no time, Ez had a pit crew helping us get ready. He was also going to teach me the performance driving school.

9

The car was finished and ready to go on the track. Ez said we would practice with starter cars first. Ez was in one car and I followed behind him in another. He was giving me instructions through a headset in my helmet. He was a great instructor and a lot of fun. I really liked him.

He taught me how to slide around corners. He also taught me how to pass. He said I learned quickly, so I switched to the lead. Then he taught me how to keep someone from passing me. This was really similar to the arcade simulator. The biggest difference was feeling the G-force going around corners.

It was a three day course. I passed with a 98% on the written test and 100% with driving. Ez jokingly said I could have passed after only one day. We filed with the IMSA the same day. I just barely made it. I got the second to last spot open for qualifying.

10

It was qualifying day, and man was I nervous. Each driver got two times around the track. Your best time determined your placement. My hands were shaky, but I wasn't giving up, not for anything. The spotters all checked in to make sure I could hear them. They were around the course to tell me how I was doing. I got out on the track and warmed up the tires. I took one lap around before they started timing me.

Green flag was out. My time started as I crossed the start/finish line. Don was at the start/finish line timing me as well. After I crossed the start/finish line, I heard Don's voice in my headset.

"Great job, Zack, but I know you can do better than that. Don't be shy on the throttle, Buddy. Punch it on the straight-a-ways. There's no one else out there to get in your way." Don's encouragement really helped. I punched it hard on the straight-a-ways and cut my time drastically.

Now, we had to wait. The others had to finish before we could hear our placement. It seemed to take forever.

Finally, they were announcing everyone's placement. I impatiently waited to hear them call my name.

"Zack Wilton, position 24, with 2:36.212."

"24th, Wahoo!" I shouted.

"Position 24! Hahaha, that's great!" Don shouted.

When they announced my position, the crowd cheered. I was starting to get a large fan base. All the news interviews had drawn people in.

11

The motorsports park was packed on the day of the race. There were even some people in the stands holding signs with my name on them. I started up the engine, to let it warm up. We checked and rechecked everything on the car. We didn't want to miss anything that might have loosened during qualifying.

All the race cars were lined up at the start/finish line. 43 cars total were in the race. The cars were in rows of two. Except for the last row, it only had one.

I suited up and got in the car. I was nervous, but I tried not to show it for my mom's sake. I could tell she was already really nervous for me.

Ez gave me a thumbs up. That meant I was all ready to go. The announcer called out over the loudspeaker, "The race is about to begin!"

All the crew members cleared the course. The flagman stepped out into position. He held up the green flag. All the drivers revved their engines.

The flagman pulled the green flag down, waving it in a figure eight. The race had begun.

12

The cars in the front started to go, one row at a time. It didn't take long for it to be my turn to go. As soon as the cars in front of me went, I took off. Suddenly, there was a crash two rows in front of me. A driver must have missed a gear. Four cars wrecked, including the car next to me and in front of me. I swerved, just missing the wreck. I instantly went from the 24th spot to 20th.

This track had some great places to pass. Don and Ez had given me some really good tips on passing. I also owned a lot of racing games. Those were actually the only games I played.

In no time, I was moving up in the ranks. First lap, I jumped two more spots forward. Two laps later, I jumped another and another spot forward.

Before I knew it, I was in 4th place. I could hardly believe it. A Mustang and Viper had taken each other out fighting over 1st and 2nd. Their crash bumped me into 4th.

The cars in front of me were really fast and aggressive. It was practically impossible for me to move forward another spot.

"You're doing great, Zack," Don said in my headset. "Just keep doing what you're doing, Bud." For the rest of the race the Porsche team had 1st and 2nd, a BMW had 3rd, and I was in 4th.

"Two more laps to go, Bud," Don said. In no time, I was passing the white flag. Last lap.

"Zack, I think the Mustang is trying to retake second. He is aggressively pushing his way forward," one of my spotters squawked in through my headset. "He's already clipped two cars and is only one car behind you now."

"Just let him pass you," Don said. "One spot in the first race isn't worth losing the car over."

The Mustang passed the car behind me. Immediately, he was right on my tail.

13

I slowed and moved to the side, letting the Mustang pass. He zoomed past me and bullied his way past the BMW in 3rd. He tried to push past the Porsche in 2nd as well.

The Porsche pushed back. The two cars spun out, taking the BMW in 3rd place with them. I swerved and missed getting caught in the wreck. Now I was in 2nd. I was only a turn from the last straight-a-way. I shot out of the curve into the straight-a-way and stomped the accelerator. The Porsche was too fast, I just couldn't pass it. The checkered flag was out. I took second.

Even though I only took second, the crowd was screaming my name. After the awards ceremony, we had a big celebration at the Wilton tent.

The TV news reporters and fans all came to the tent.

The first question I was asked was from Kim Sutherland, "How does it feel to go from hero to racer?"

That one I knew the answer to right away, "It feels good. Really good."

AFTER

Don left his office job and went into racing. He is now a top paid advisor in the motorsports field. Zack went on to win the championship as the overall points leader. He is now driving for more than one style of racing.

About The Author

"I was once a struggling reader, just like you. I had neurological damage after having an allergic reaction. It took me years and years of hard work and never giving up, for me to be where I am today. Keep pushing on, no matter how hard it is, and you will be able to accomplish anything."

~Matthias Southwick

About The Publisher

Story Shares is a nonprofit focused on supporting the millions of teens and adults who struggle with reading by creating a new shelf in the library specifically for them. The ever-growing collection features content that is compelling and culturally relevant for teens and adults, yet still readable at a range of lower reading levels.

Story Shares generates content by engaging deeply with writers, bringing together a community to create this new kind of book. With more intriguing and approachable stories to choose from, the teens and adults who have fallen behind are improving their skills and beginning to discover the joy of reading. For more information, visit storyshares.org.

Easy to Read. Hard to Put Down.

www.ingramcontent.com/pod-product-compliance
Lightning Source LLC
Chambersburg PA
CBHW071229170626
46809CB00005BA/1981